Wendell

Eric Jon Nones

Farrar, Straus and Giroux

New York

"Wendell, what's gotten into you! Get down off that counter this minute."

"Mom, how come there are only two forks here?
I can't set the table with just two forks."
"Well, I put out three just a minute ago. Let me see."

"There *are* three forks here, plain as the nose on your face. Wendell, I told you before, stay off my counters! Get down!"

"Look, Mom, this plate is cracked. But I didn't do it."
"I'm sure you didn't, dear. Wendell probably did it."

"Now, where are my glasses? I always leave them right here. Honey, have you seen my glasses?"

"I don't wear them, dear. Where'd you put them last?"
"Well, I could have sworn I left them here by my chair.
You don't suppose Wendell got them?"

"Wendell! Have you gone crazy?"
"My glasses! I knew Wendell had them. You good-
for-nothing cat. You're going out for the night."

"What crummy reception. I bet Wendell is up on the roof right now playing with the antenna."

"I wouldn't be surprised."

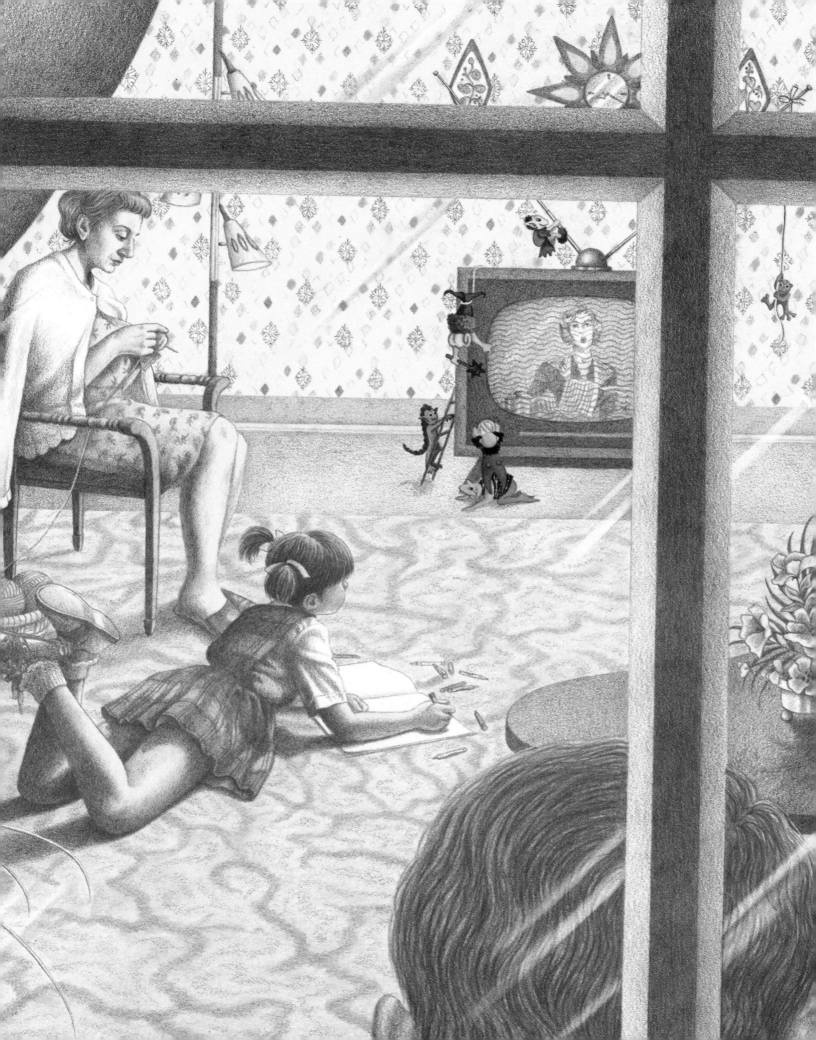

"Now, why on earth do you suppose the light is flicking on and off like that?"

"I don't know, but it's giving me a headache. I'm getting some aspirin. Darned slipper. Where's it hiding?"

"I can't find the aspirin."
"It couldn't have just got up and walked away.
I suppose we ran out. Just come to bed."

"Where's Wendell?"
"He's still outside, Dad."

"Oh, my gosh! A mouse!"
"Get it out!"
"I'll let Wendell in."

"Get 'em, Wendell, get 'em."
"Thank goodness."
"Go to it, Wendell old boy!"

"Wendell, our hero."

"Fine job, Wendell. That's the way to scare off the little devil."

"Wendell, you dear sweet puss. What would we ever do without you!"

Wendell had to agree.